Big Fright

D0048972

With special thanks to Jim Collins

First published in Great Britain in 2012 by Buster Books,
an imprint of Michael O'Mara Books Limited,
9 Lion Yard, Tremadoc Road, London SW4 7NQ

www.busterbooks.co.uk
www.monstrousmaud.co.uk

Series created by Working Partners Limited
Text copyright © Working Partners Limited 2012

Cover design by Nicola Theobald

Illustration copyright © Buster Books 2012
Illustrations by Sarah Horne

A CIP catalogue record for this book is available
from the British Library.

ISBN: 978-1-78055-072-5 in paperback print format
ISBN: 978-1-78055-082-4 in Epub format
ISBN: 978-1-78055-083-1 in Mobipocket format

1 3 5 7 9 10 8 6 4 2

Papers used by Michael O'Mara Books are natural,
recyclable products made from wood grown in sustainable forests.
The manufacturing processes conform to the environmental
regulations of the country of origin.

Printed and bound in March 2012 by CPI Group (UK) Ltd,
108 Beddington Lane, Croydon, CR0 4YY, United Kingdom.

Big Fright

A. B. Saddlewick

BUSTER

Chapter One

Maud didn't know how much more she could sit through.

It was the last lesson of the day at Primrose Towers, and the girls were showing off their craft projects. Each one was more boring than the last. Sometimes Maud thought her classmates were from a different planet. Or maybe she was the alien one …

Poppy Simpkins had knitted a tiny pink cardigan for her teddy bear. Sarah Wentworth had flipped through endless pages of flower pressings. Daffodils, daisies, bluebells, violets.

She hadn't even collected any interesting plants like poison ivy or Venus flytraps.

Maud Montague patted the top of her ice-cream tub, checking that none of the air-holes were covered up, and waited for her turn. She had something much more exciting to show than tedious teddies or floppy flowers. Something the whole class was going to love.

Miss Bloom glanced around. "Now let's hear from …"

Maud leaned forward.

"… Milly."

Drat, thought Maud. Milly Montague was her twin sister, and you could bet your eyeballs that whatever she'd brought in would be even more soppy than dried flowers and teddy clothes put together.

Milly skipped up to the front, and Maud wondered what she was about to pull out of her pink backpack. She had refused to tell Maud on the school bus that morning. Would it be a fluffy unicorn made from rose petals? A rainbow-coloured friendship bracelet?

It turned out to be even worse. Milly produced a white cardboard box, opened it and offered it to Miss Bloom. Inside Maud could see an enormous pink cake, with the words "Best Teacher Ever" written on it in purple icing.

Her classmates clapped with joy.

Maud frowned. Weren't they supposed to have made interesting things? So where were the wormeries and monster costumes and jars of fungus-sprouting jam?

"Three cheers for Miss Bloom," shouted Milly. "Hip, hip …"

"Hooray!" shouted everyone except Maud.

"Thank you," said Miss Bloom. "Another excellent contribution, Milly. I'd give you a gold star, but you've used them all up."

Maud rolled her eyes. If they thought the cake was so special, just wait until they saw what she'd made.

"Who's next?" Miss Bloom looked around and sighed. "Well, I suppose everyone else has had their turn. It's got to be Maud."

The other pupils groaned.

"Not Monstrous Maud!" shouted Poppy, from her desk at the front.

"I hope this is better than the dead bug collection," said Alice Jones.

"Please don't let her talk about maggots again," said Suzie Singh. "We've just had lunch."

Sarah put a trembling hand up. "Can I go to the toilet please, Miss?"

"Hold on for a minute," said Miss Bloom. "Let's get this over with."

Maud stepped up to the front of the class with her plastic tub. "Today I've brought my pet," she said. "His name's Quentin."

Suzie cowered behind her hands as Maud opened the ice-cream tub.

Inside was a rock, with a tiny scrap of black cloth attached to it.

Poppy stood on tiptoes and peered into the tub. "You have a pet rock? With a cape? Called Quentin?"

"I told you she was a weirdo," said Sarah.

"Quentin's not a rock," said Maud. "He must have escaped."

The girls shuffled around in discomfort.

"It's nothing to worry about," Maud added. "It's only *wild* rats that carry diseases."

All the girls in the class jumped up on to their chairs and began to scream. All the girls except Milly. She was sitting quietly behind her desk, with her pens arranged in neat rows and a spiteful smile on her lips. It was the smile she kept for the times when she got Maud into trouble.

Maud didn't have time to worry about her sister, though. She had to calm the class down and find Quentin.

"Please could you stop screaming?" she asked. "Quentin's very nervous around new people." It was no use. She couldn't even hear herself above the terrified shrieks.

Miss Bloom stepped forward from her desk and shouted over the din. "Be quiet!" In an instant, the class was silent. "Miss Montague is clearly playing another of her ridiculous jokes!"

Maud noticed that the papers on Miss Bloom's desk were moving. Underneath them she spotted a long, black tail flicking back and forth.

"Er, Miss Bloom ..." she began.

The papers moved again, and Quentin scuttled out from under them to the front of the desk, his claws rattling on the wooden surface. His grey fur was even messier than normal where he'd been rummaging; it stood up in tufts all over his body. He lifted himself on to his hind legs and inspected the class with a curious glint in his pink eyes. The girls froze, staring wide-eyed at the rat.

"You've caused quite enough havoc for

one day," said Miss Bloom, who hadn't seen Quentin yet.

"But Miss …"

"But nothing. Stand outside and think about what you've done!" Miss Bloom turned to the class. "And as for the rest of you, get off those chairs at once!"

Maud was about to scoop Quentin up and leave the room when the rat scurried to the edge of the desk and jumped off. He landed on Miss Bloom's skirt, latching on with his claws. The class wailed with a single voice of terror.

"What …?" muttered the teacher, twirling on the spot to get a look. Quentin squeaked in panic, scampered around her back and disappeared up her jumper. Now Miss Bloom screamed too and writhed about, arms flapping in a wild dance.

"Stay still, Miss!" said Maud.

Her teacher froze and a second later Quentin's nose peered out of the neck of the jumper. Miss Bloom turned her head slowly, eyes widening as they lit on the rat. Maud saw Quentin smile back, his little yellow teeth peeping over his bottom lip.

Miss Bloom opened her mouth to speak, but no words came out. Her knees started to wobble. Maud rushed forward to pluck Quentin off her shoulder. By the time Maud had him clutched safely to her chest, Miss Bloom had fainted in a heap on the floor.

Chapter Two

Fifteen minutes later, Maud stood in Mrs Fennel's office.

She'd been here a billion times before. Mrs Fennel always sat behind her perfectly tidy desk in her perfectly neat blouse and gave Maud a stern telling off. Then she warned her never to do it again and let her leave. It wasn't that bad, really.

"Maud Montague," Mrs Fennel began. "This is unacceptable! It's worse than the time you poured green food dye in the baked beans. It's even worse than the wolf mask incident."

Maud couldn't believe Mrs Fennel was still going on about that mask. How was Maud to know the caretaker got scared so easily? She hadn't expected him to throw down his mop and flee out of the gates in terror.

"It was meant to be a joke," she explained.

"I'm not sure Mr Carter saw it that way," said Mrs Fennel. "He needed a whole month off to recover. And now this. I shouldn't have to tell you, Maud, that rats are not allowed in the classroom. It's just not … proper."

Mrs Fennel was obsessed with things being proper. Everything in the school, from pens to pupils, had to be in the correct place at the correct time, doing exactly what they were supposed to do.

"Quentin's not a fearsome sort of rat," said Maud. "If anything he's too shy for his own good. It's the rest of the class that should be in trouble. If they hadn't frightened him with their screams, we would have found him sooner."

"I'm sorry, Maud, but I won't listen to any more of your excuses. It's time we faced facts. We've tried and tried with you, but it just isn't working. Miss Bloom is going to have to take time off to recover, and the school can't afford to lose more staff. I'm going to have to ask you to leave Primrose Towers."

Leave? Maud couldn't believe it. She wasn't being told to say sorry. She wasn't being told not to do it again. She was being expelled!

"But …"

"I'm sorry, Maud, but I see no alternative."

Before Maud could say anything more, Mrs Fennel picked up her phone and dialled. "Hello, it's Felicity Fennel here. Yes, from Primrose Towers. I was wondering if you could help me. I'm looking to transfer a pupil named Maud Montague."

Maud listened in disbelief. Was Mrs Fennel allowed to do this?

"Her behaviour?" said Mrs Fennel. "Oh, it's

dreadful. Quite the worst I've ever known. The things she gets up to ... well, I'm sure you'll find out. Excellent. Thank you."

Mrs Fennel put down the phone and smiled with her eyes closed as though she was slipping into a warm bath. "Good news," she said. "That was the headmistress at Rotwood School. She says she'll take you."

Maud was puzzled. "I'm surprised she wanted me after that description."

"Nonsense. I think you'll fit in perfectly."

As Mrs Fennel spoke, a smile seemed to be tugging at her lips.

"I'll let your parents know you can start on Monday. The school's in the middle of the forest to the north of Sommerton, and you can get a bus there from your usual stop."

"How will I know which bus to ..."

"You won't miss it. I can assure you of that."

Maud thought that a creepy forest sounded like a strange place for a school. Still, it had to be more interesting than Primrose Towers.

"All right," she said. "I'll go."

Mrs Fennel narrowed her eyes as she peered across her pristine desk. "I wasn't offering you a choice."

After that, Maud went back to the classroom to fetch Quentin. "It's a shame the others didn't get to see you in your little cape," she whispered to him. "You would have made a brilliant vampire rat." Quentin's nose twitched, as if he agreed with her.

As Maud was on her way down the corridor to leave Primrose Towers for the last time, she heard a commotion in the staffroom. It sounded like laughing, cheering and … was that a party popper being let off? *They must be celebrating something*, thought Maud … although she had no idea what.

Maud glared at her sister as they sat around the dinner table that night. "You shouldn't have let him out! He was absolutely terrified. He could have been squashed in all the panic."

"I don't know what you mean," said Milly. "I didn't do anything. It's not my fault you got into trouble and ended up getting expelled. Tell her, Mum."

Mrs Montague looked up from the script she was reading and adjusted her large round glasses. "You mustn't say your sister was expelled, cupcake. She was transferred." She looked back down at the script and continued eating her dinner. Spaghetti sauce was splashing all over her cream-coloured jumper, but she was so engrossed in the script that she didn't seem to notice. For the last few weeks, she'd been designing costumes for the local amateur dramatic society's production of *Dracula – The Musical*, and it was hard to talk to her about anything else.

Mr Montague looked up from his copy of *Vintage Car Magazine*, his eyes huge behind the lenses in his glasses. "And you mustn't say your sister was transferred as a punishment. The headmistress simply said that Maud would fit in better at Rotwood."

He pointed at a picture in his magazine. "It's like this Volvo P1800. You could put the engine from a V70 into it, but it wouldn't run. That doesn't make one right and the other wrong. It just means they're different."

Here we go again, thought Maud. Her dad always found a way to bring things round to cars. As he droned on about different types of engines, she glared back at Milly.

Milly smiled sweetly, as though she couldn't understand what the problem was. When their dad was busy reading again, Milly winked at Maud. Her smile changed from angelic to mean.

That settled it. It *had* been Milly who let Quentin out of his ice-cream tub!

Later that night, Maud popped into the garage to check on Quentin. She didn't like him being out here on his own. Her parents let him come in the house during the day, but Milly had kicked up a massive fuss about having 'vermin' in the bedroom while she slept. Although that didn't stop Maud sneaking him in when it was really cold. Maud thought it was very unfair, because Lollipop, Milly's rabbit, was allowed to live in the utility room and sometimes even slept on Milly's beanbag. Maud reached inside and stroked the rat's head.

"Sorry about my sister," she said.

Quentin shuddered, as if he was thinking about Milly.

Okay, so his fur was a bit patchy in places, but that wasn't his fault. When she'd first found

Quentin, trapped in one of their bins, he was thin and wet and scared. Maud thought he'd been in a fight with a local cat. She'd fed him up over the next few weeks, and now he had doubled in size and was much more confident.

"Milly was very mean to let you loose like that," she said. "But you're safe now, and that's the main thing."

Maud placed a blanket over Quentin's cage and was just about to leave when she spotted something in the corner of the garage – a caterpillar nest. She watched as the tiny insects squirmed around it, crawling under and over each other. It looked like a huge rotten ball of candyfloss, teeming with activity.

Even better, the caterpillars had spun their nest around a pile of twigs, so she was able to pick up the entire thing and take it to her room. She could even show it to Milly. Perhaps sharing something as cool as this would help them put the Quentin incident behind them. Of course,

Milly had started it. But if Maud was nice to her, maybe she wouldn't do something like this again.

Maud carried the nest upstairs carefully to the bedroom she shared with her sister. It was a strange-looking room, thanks to an argument they'd had while choosing wallpaper. In the end, their dad had decided that Milly should choose the decoration for her half of the room, and Maud should choose the decoration for hers. As a result, Maud's half was covered in spooky black wallpaper, with brilliant glow-in-the-dark spider stickers, and Milly's half was covered in sugar pink wallpaper, on which were pinned drawings of fairies, rainbows and magical castles.

The bunk bed that Maud shared with her sister was against the wall in the middle of the room, where the black and pink wallpapers met. Milly had insisted on taking the top bunk, so Maud had to make do with the bottom one.

But she didn't mind because the gap underneath it made an excellent space for Quentin's daytime den of twigs and branches and old pieces of cardboard boxes.

Milly was lying underneath the frilly pink duvet on her bunk, reading her *Bumper Book of Pony Stories*.

"Look at this," said Maud. "Isn't it cool?" She lifted the writhing nest up to her sister, who jerked upright and screamed.

"Mum!" Milly shouted. "Maud's throwing insects at me again."

"Don't throw insects at your sister, dear," came their mum's voice from downstairs.

"I wasn't throwing them," said Maud, carefully placing the nest under the bottom bunk. "I was showing them to you. I just thought you might be interested."

"How many times do I have to tell you?" asked Milly. "I'm not interested in worms or spiders or creepy-crawlies of any kind.

And even if I was, I wouldn't want the filthy things in my bedroom."

As Milly chattered on about how disgusting it was to bring insects into the house, Maud changed into her pyjamas and threw her clothes on to the floor. On her side of the room, the floor was completely covered with rumpled clothes, spooky books and scary Halloween masks. On Milly's side, the floor was spotless, with all her possessions stowed away neatly in her lilac chest of drawers.

Maud crawled under her black duvet. Above her, Milly was still complaining.

"I can't imagine how many germs you must have brought in. You'd better make sure you don't touch any of my things."

Maud wondered what was wrong with her sister. Didn't she like anything interesting? She closed her eyes. While she waited for sleep to come, her mind kept wandering, thinking about her new school. What was it going to be like? Only the weekend to go, and then she would find out.

Chapter Three

On Monday morning, Maud woke up early to pack her bag. It was pouring with rain outside – Maud's favourite sort of weather – and she was very excited about her new school. But she couldn't help feeling a little nervous too. What if nobody spoke to her? What if it was just like Primrose Towers? In the end, she decided to take Quentin along in the pocket of her blazer, so she'd have at least one friend. Then she waited by the front door for her sister. She'd wanted to leave early to make sure she didn't miss the Rotwood bus, but her parents had insisted she walked to the stop with Milly as usual.

Maud's parents hadn't been able to buy the Rotwood uniform yet, so she was still wearing the navy-blue uniform of Primrose Towers. She hoped it wouldn't look too strange to the other pupils.

"Are you ready yet?" shouted Maud.

Milly stormed out on to the landing. "How can I go when I can't find my tutu? What have you done with it?"

Maud shrugged. She had no idea where it was.

"Well, I've got a big show on Friday, and I can't practise without it, so you're going to have to wait." Milly stomped back into their room.

A couple of minutes later, she emerged holding the frilly pink ballet tutu.

"What a surprise!" she shouted. "It was under a pile of stinky clothes on your side of the room. Now it's covered in Maud germs and

I don't have time to wash it."

"I didn't touch it," said Maud. "You must have thrown it there after your last ballet lesson."

"No," said Milly. "You're the one who leaves clothes on the floor. I fold them and put them back in my drawers."

Even after they'd finally said goodbye to their parents and set out for the bus stop, Milly kept chattering about her tutu. She glared at Maud from under her umbrella.

"Admit it," she said. "You hid my tutu on purpose. You hid it because you're jealous that I was chosen for the ballet performance on Friday and you weren't."

"How could I have been chosen?" asked Maud. "I didn't audition."

The Primrose Towers bus pulled up at the stop just as they arrived. Through the spotless windows, Maud could see the rows of girls in their perfectly ironed uniforms. She was glad she didn't have to get on the bus today, especially as it would mean listening to more of Milly's boasting about her starring role in the ballet.

"Smell you later," said Milly, as she stepped on to the bus. "Have a nice time with the Rotwood rejects." She shook out her umbrella, covering Maud in spray.

The door closed, and the bus drove off before Maud could reply. Never mind. She wasn't too bothered about Milly's taunts – she was too busy wondering about her new school in the creepy forest.

Whenever the Montague family went for a walk, their dad had always insisted they avoid the forest. He said it was dark and gloomy, with no proper paths to walk along.

But Maud was sure it was fine. Mrs Fennel wouldn't have transferred her to somewhere dangerous, would she?

Maud looked down the road for the bus. It should have been here by now. She hoped she hadn't missed it while Milly was looking for her tutu.

While she was waiting, she took a letter out of her bag. It was from the head teacher of Rotwood. It had arrived on Saturday morning, and was entirely different from any letter they'd ever received from Primrose Towers. Whenever Mrs Fennel had written to complain about Maud's behaviour, it had always been printed on headed A4 paper and folded neatly. But this letter was scrawled in spidery handwriting on what looked like ancient yellow parchment, and sealed with green wax. It had a funny smell, too. A cross between mouldy bread and her dad's stinkiest trainers, Maud thought.

Dear Mr and Mrs Montague,

We are delighted to hear that Maud will be joining us as a new pupil on Monday. I have arranged for her to be picked up by the school bus at 8:30a.m. and she has been allocated to Class 3B. From what we've heard about Maud, it sounds as if she'll be perfect for us, and I'm certain she'll have a terrifying time.

Yours,

The Head

Maud wrinkled her nose. That couldn't be right. Surely it meant "a terrific time". The handwriting was very unclear. If Maud had written so badly at Primrose Towers, she would have been given a detention.

Maud heard a loud spluttering and looked up. A bus – if you could call it that – stood right in front of her. It was more of a misshapen lump of rusty metal than a vehicle, with thick black smoke pumping out of the exhaust and windows that were so dirty you couldn't see in. It had **ROTWOOD SCHOOL** painted on the side in black letters.

The door creaked open on its loose hinges and Maud stepped on, wondering how safe the bus could possibly be.

"Hello," she said to the driver. She didn't want to stare, but he looked so weird she couldn't help herself. He was tall and thin, with a long pale face and dark, hollow eyes. He was crammed into the narrow driver's seat so tightly that he had to reach around his knees to get to the wheel. It reminded Maud of watching a daddy-long-legs try to crawl into a matchbox.

The driver grunted, which Maud took as a sign that she should find a seat. She peered down the gloomy bus, but all the seats looked occupied. Down the aisle, Maud could see pupils who were bundled up in bulky hooded coats, wrapped in thick scarves or shielded by large hats with wide brims. And the weird thing was that it wasn't even very cold. If they dressed like this in September, they'd probably be wearing Arctic exploring gear by Christmas.

The bus lurched and grunted into action. Rain hammered off the windows. As her eyes adjusted to the dark, Maud made her way down the aisle. She felt as if every pair of eyes was watching her.

She spotted an empty seat near the back. Dark red stains covered the fabric, and huge chunks of stuffing had been ripped out of it, but Maud was so pleased to escape the glares of the pupils that she didn't mind.

Maud looked at the boy sitting next to her.

Like everyone else on the bus, he was bizarrely overdressed, in a large raincoat and baseball cap. When he pulled the brim of the cap down over his eyes, Maud thought he was wearing large furry gloves. But, on closer inspection, she saw that he actually had very hairy hands.

Maud tried to smile at him, but he turned to look out of the window. She saw he had hair all over the back of his neck too. She hoped he didn't get teased about it too much.

Maud looked around the bus and saw that the hairy boy wasn't the only unusual one. A boy wearing a balaclava seemed to have green skin underneath. There was a girl with a long, hooked nose. Another girl hid behind massive sunglasses. What sort of school was this?

Maud was glad that she had Quentin with her. She took him out of her blazer pocket and stroked his fur. Quentin glanced round at the pupils, then scuttled right back into her pocket. Maud knew how he felt.

"Aww, he's monstrous! Big, too!"

Maud was surprised to see the hairy boy staring at her rat. She was even more surprised that he seemed to like Quentin so much. It was a bit odd that he'd called Quentin 'monstrous', but still. She'd have needed a litter of golden Labrador puppies to get a reaction like that in Primrose Towers.

"Thanks," said Maud. "He's my pet."

"I always wanted a pet," said the hairy boy. "But Dad said it would be too much effort not to feed on it."

"Don't you mean 'it would be too much effort to feed it'?" asked Maud.

"Er, yeah, if you say so," said the boy.

A moment later, things got even darker inside the bus. Maud peered out and saw that they'd entered the forest. The trees had grown so thick that it seemed as if they were in a tunnel, and the driver had to turn his lights on. A dark shape scuttled among the trees, and Maud felt a shiver run down her spine.

The bus let out a loud splutter and Maud prayed it wouldn't break down. She didn't like the idea of having to get out and wait for someone to come and fix it.

Soon the bus emerged into a large clearing in the wood, and Maud could see a little more clearly. Up ahead, she spotted a faded sign:

BECAUSE WE SCARE

Some vandal had obviously changed 'care' to 'scare' for a joke. It almost looked as if that's what the sign was supposed to say, though.

The bus chugged to a stop.

"Everybody out," said the driver in a strange, croaky voice.

The pupils crowded off, causing the bus to rock up and down violently. Maud followed them, eager to get her first look at Rotwood.

Chapter Four

The rain had eased off, leaving a thin mist in the air.

Maud stepped off the bus and looked up at Rotwood School. It seemed more like a ruined castle than a school. Instead of modern red bricks, it was built from ancient blocks of grey stone. Leering gargoyles peered down from the corners of the roof. Instead of large windows, it had small arched openings, some blocked by weather-beaten shutters. And rather than a swooshing glass door surrounded by noticeboards and potted trees, a heavy oak door opened into a dark entrance hall.

Maud realised she had no idea where she was going. She checked her letter and called over to the hairy boy. "Excuse me, do you know how I get to Class 3B?"

The boy smiled. "That's my class! I'll show you the way. It's strange, Batty didn't mention anything about a new girl."

Now that they were out of the darkness inside the bus, Maud could see that the boy's face was covered entirely in hair. His cheeks, his nose and even his forehead all sprouted thick brown fur. She wanted to ask if he'd heard of shaving foam, but then decided she'd better not upset him.

She followed the hairy boy into the school. At first she thought there must have been some sort of power cut, because she could see nothing at all. But as her eyes adjusted, she found that she was actually in a vast entrance hall, lit by just a few candles.

Maud loved the dark. She was always getting into trouble with her sister for leaving their bedroom curtains closed on sunny days. But she was still surprised by the murkiness of the school, and the pupils scuttling around in the half-light.

There was a very odd smell in the entrance hall, too. Everything reeked of damp dustiness, like the garage her dad escaped to at weekends to tinker with his car parts. At Primrose Towers, Mrs Fennel had insisted the corridors were sprayed with lilac air-freshener three times a day. A whiff of this place would probably kill her.

Twisty corridors led out of the hall in all directions, and two wide stone staircases at either side climbed up into darkness. There were no signposts or maps, and Maud was glad she had the hairy boy to show her the way.

"We're up here," the boy said, pointing at a spiral staircase through a narrow doorway.

Maud followed him up the steps, higher and higher, moving so fast she got dizzy. In some places the candles had burned right down to waxy stumps, leaving the stairwell in pitch blackness, but she pushed onwards.

At the top, the hairy boy led her into a large classroom filled with old-fashioned wooden chairs and desks. On one side of the room, three arched windows looked out on the damp morning. On the opposite wall was a huge scroll showing a family tree, which looked far too old and valuable to be hanging up in a classroom.

All around them, pupils were taking off their coats, scarves and hats. But instead of looking more normal without their extra layers, they looked even weirder. The boy she'd followed didn't just have hair on his face. It was all over his neck and arms, and possibly underneath his shirt too. He looked more as if he belonged in a kennel than a classroom. She saw a girl from the bus who had a pea-sized wart right on the end of her hooked nose. Her straggly hair was dyed purple, and she was putting on a large pointed hat to go with her ragged black dress. Maud wondered why she was wearing a witch costume on a Monday morning in September. Could she be going to an early Halloween party? At school?

The girl with the gigantic sunglasses took them off and glared at Maud. Maud looked away. Those weren't the kind of eyes you wanted to stare back at. They were bright red.

Next to Maud, a boy took off his baseball cap to reveal a novelty headband. There was a pair of small fake horns sticking out of it – except they didn't look very fake at all.

Maud wondered if she'd been wrong about the pupils. Maybe they weren't wearing extra layers for warmth. Maybe they were wearing them for … disguise?

It was better not to think about it. Maud wanted to make a good impression on her new classmates. She didn't want to stand around gawping at them, however odd they were.

$*\ ^* *\ * \ *\ *\ *\ \ ^*$

Maud found a spare locker at the back of the classroom to put her bag in. Then she scooped Quentin out of her blazer pocket and put him inside, too. "Don't worry, you'll be safe in here," she whispered to the trembling rat. She found an empty chair and tried to pull it out.

"Er, hello? This seat is taken!"

Maud looked around to see where the voice had come from, but there was no one there.

"Sorry," she said, and moved to the next desk, beside the hairy boy.

"No one ever notices me," grumbled the voice. "I'm sick of it."

Maud was still trying to work out who was speaking when the teacher strode into the classroom. He was unlike any teacher Maud had ever seen. He was wearing a long black cape with blood-red lining, and his hair was slicked back perfectly. Maud couldn't wait to tell her mum about him. Maybe he should try out for the role of Count Dracula in her musical. It would certainly save a bomb on costumes.

Maud giggled, and the teacher glared at her.

"A classroom is not a place for laughter," he said. "Perhaps you'd like to tell us all what you find so amusing?"

"Nothing," said Maud. "I was just thinking how much you look like Dracula."

The teacher's glare turned into a scowl, and the entire room fell silent. Maud wondered if she'd said the wrong thing.

"Do not mention the name of that ridiculous

show-off in this classroom," he said. "You're here to learn, not to talk about silly attention-seekers who give the rest of us a bad name."

"Sorry."

"I certainly hope you are. My name is Mr Von Bat. I take it you're the new pupil?"

"Yes, Sir. I'm Maud Montague."

There were titters from the other pupils, as if that was funny.

"Maud Montague. How odd. Well, Maud, you're lucky we had a spare place at Rotwood. What happened to Bertie was unfortunate."

Maud was about to ask the hairy boy what this meant, but he shook his head.

"You don't want to know," he whispered.

Mr Von Bat opened his desk drawer and brought out a folder, a feather quill and an inkpot. He dipped the quill. "Let's see who's here. Poisonous Penelope?"

"Here," said the girl with the pointed hat.

"Invisible Isabel?"

And they thought Maud's name was funny!

"Here," came a voice from the empty chair next to Maud.

"Wilf?" continued the teacher.

The hairy boy let out a howl that made the rest of the class giggle.

"Save it for the full moon," said Mr Von Bat. "You don't have long to wait." He looked back at the page. "Vladimir Paprika Wellington Counterweight Von Bat?"

There was no reply. Mr Von Bat sighed, looking at an empty chair by the window. "That boy's always—"

Something smacked right into the glass of the window outside and slid down the pane. Maud couldn't be sure, but it looked suspiciously like a bat.

Wilf leapt up and opened the window. A huge puff of smoke billowed into the room and a small, pale boy fell out of it and collapsed on the floor.

He stood up and dusted himself down. Like Mr Von Bat, he was wearing a black cape with red lining.

"Sorry, Dad," he said.

Mr Von Bat frowned.

"I mean … Sir." The boy's hair flopped down over his forehead, and he tried to smooth it back.

"Sit down at once, Vladimir," said Mr Von Bat. "And next time you feel like shape-shifting in front of everyone, at least try to land a little more gracefully."

"Yes, Sir."

Maud looked at Vladimir with astonishment. A minute ago he'd been a bat. Now he was a boy. A rather small and timid boy, perhaps, but a boy nonetheless.

It was impossible. But she'd seen it happen.

Maud looked around the room as the truth sank in. Wilf didn't just have unruly facial hair. Isabel wasn't just throwing her voice. And

Penelope wasn't just wearing a witch costume.

A werewolf, an invisible girl and a witch …
Rotwood wasn't a school for pupils who behaved
like monsters. It was a school for pupils who
were monsters!

Chapter Five

No wonder Mrs Fennel had smiled when she'd said Maud would fit in! She must have known all about this place.

Maud looked around at the pupils. She had thought the boy at the back of the room was just very skinny. But, on closer inspection, it turned out he was a skeleton. She'd thought the boy next to him just had very bad skin. But looking again, she saw that he was a zombie with rotting grey flesh.

In front of the skeleton and zombie was a boy who looked like he was in costume for a

Shakespeare play, complete with ruff, doublet and hose. Well, at least there was one normal kid – even if he was dressed a little strangely.

"Achoo!" the boy sneezed, and his head dropped off his shoulders and rolled along the floor.

"Sorry," said his disembodied head, as his body stooped to pick it up.

Maud gasped, but nobody else seemed to think anything was out of the ordinary, so she tried to hide her surprise.

As the young vampire Vladimir fumbled into his seat, Mr Von Bat said, "I'm making a note of your lateness. That's the fifth time in two weeks."

Maud thought Mr Von Bat was being very stern with his own son. Maybe he just didn't want to look like he was treating him differently.

"If it happens again," said Mr Von Bat. "I shall be sending you to see the Head."

There was an intake of breath at the mention

of the Head. Maud thought the Head must be very frightening indeed to scare this lot.

"If you get sent to the Head, you're in real trouble," whispered Wilf. "And you have to be careful, because the Head's always watching." He shuddered and looked over his shoulder.

"Silence!" shouted Mr Von Bat. "Now if you'll all take out your History scrolls ..."

The pupils groaned as they took yellowing rolls of parchment out of their bags. Maud took out the exercise book she'd used for History lessons at Primrose Towers. She was glad she'd covered it with spooky pumpkin stickers – it didn't look too out of place.

"Don't worry," whispered Wilf. "We only have normal lessons like Vampire History, Graveyard Studies and Potion Science in the mornings. We have Fright Classes in the afternoons."

"What are Fright Classes?" asked Maud.

"Lessons in scaring people, of course. You

must have had them at your last school."

"Of course," said Maud. "But we called it, er ... 'scare science' there."

Luckily, Wilf seemed convinced.

Maud couldn't wait for the afternoon now. Fright Classes sounded like a lot of fun. She'd always enjoyed making her sister and her parents jump out of their skins by shouting, "Boo!" – and now she was going to be taught how to scare by a genuine monster. You could bet your eyeballs it would be more interesting than any of Miss Bloom's dull lessons.

Mr Von Bat walked over to the huge family tree hanging on the wall. "Now, as you'll remember from last week's lesson, the ancient vampire line of the Bitesworthys are distantly related to the Bludhaus-Essenbergs, who were descended from the great Fangston-Goryvitch dynasty ..."

It was very difficult to follow, but Maud tried to jot it down as best she could. It was hardly surprising, really. She hadn't even known that vampires were real until a few minutes ago. No wonder it was all proving a little overwhelming.

After Mr Von Bat had been explaining the family tree for an hour, a distant bell sounded, and all the pupils packed away their scrolls and filed outside for break. Maud was about to follow them when Mr Von Bat's voice stopped her.

"Not you, Miss Montague. I think you and I should have a word."

He crossed the stone floor and closed the door, leaving just the two of them in the classroom.

"If it's about the Dracula thing, I really didn't mean it," said Maud.

"Yes, well, let's try to move on from that rather unfortunate incident. It was your little secret that I wanted to talk about."

Maud wondered what secret Mr Von Bat meant. She'd once used Milly's Barbie hairbrush to comb Quentin's fur, but there's no way he could know about that.

"What secret?" she asked.

"That you're human, of course!" Mr Von Bat exploded. "That you don't have a supernatural bone in your body. You're not invisible, you can't turn into a bat, and I'm sure you've never even tasted blood. You're just a normal little girl, and yet you've got the cheek to turn up at a school that's strictly for monsters only!"

Maud's heart sank. "How did you know?"

"I've been teaching monsters for years, and I know a fake when I see one. And what I'm looking at now is an ordinary little girl."

Maud didn't like being called ordinary. She didn't see why she couldn't be just as spooky as all the others if she tried her best. Even if she was human.

"I'm going to talk to the Head about you," said Mr Von Bat. "I fully expect you'll be sent back to your old school."

Maud thought about Primrose Towers. No way did she want to go back to its clean corridors and prissy pupils. Rotwood might be very freaky and even a little frightening, but at least it was interesting.

"Please don't tell the Head!" said Maud. "My old school was stuffy and boring. I don't want to be sent back!"

Mr Von Bat considered this for a moment and then chuckled to himself. "Very well," he said. "If you're so keen to stay, I'll give you until the end of the week. If you can scare me by Friday, I won't take the matter any further."

Maud let out a huge sigh of relief.

"Oh, I wouldn't get too excited," said Mr Von Bat. "I ought to warn you that I'm completely, one-hundred-per-cent fright proof."

Chapter Six

As Maud made her way back down the gloomy staircase, she thought about Mr Von Bat's challenge. What could she do to frighten a bloodsucking vampire like him? It seemed impossible, but she had to try. If she got expelled again, Milly would never let her forget it.

At the bottom of the staircase, Maud followed a group of pupils through the main hall. They trooped out of a large stone doorway at the back that had the word **PLAYGROUND** engraved above it.

A grassy area stretched out behind the school, in which uneven grey slabs of stone seemed to have been planted. They were covered in damp moss and shrouded by thick swirls of mist. It took Maud a moment to realise she was in a graveyard. The pupils wove in and out of tombs, playing tag. It wasn't like any playground Maud had ever seen before.

Maud spotted Wilf and Mr Von Bat's son in an overgrown part of the graveyard, playing catch with the head of the boy who looked as if he was from a Shakespeare play. Maud thought they were being mean for a moment, then realised that the boy's head was smiling.

"Hi Maud!" said Vladimir. "I'm Paprika."

"I thought you were Vladimir."

"My dad calls me that when I'm in trouble."

"Hi Maud!" said the disembodied head, just as Wilf caught it. "I'm Oscar."

"Er ... hi," said Maud.

Wilf threw Oscar's head back towards

Paprika. Unfortunately, it slipped through the vampire's fingers and landed in a patch of long grass.

"Oops," said Paprika. "Sorry."

"Butterfingers!" shouted Oscar's head, as Paprika ran over to fetch it. Somebody tapped Maud on the shoulder and she turned to see that it was Oscar's headless body. He held his hand out and she shook it nervously. She didn't quite know where to look, so she just smiled at where Oscar's face should have been.

"Pleased to meet you," said Oscar's head. "And thanks for being scared of me. That's very nice of you."

"Hey, new girl!" shouted a voice from across the graveyard.

It was Poisonous Penelope, the witch from Maud's class. She strode over, a werewolf at her side. The werewolf must have been at least two-metres tall, with thick whiskers sprouting around his nose and sharp teeth jutting from his gums.

"Hey," said Wilf to the larger werewolf, and Maud noticed that his voice shook a little.

The big werewolf just growled in reply.

"What's the matter with you, new girl?" asked Poisonous Penelope. "You look like you've never seen a ghost."

Maud tried to laugh this off. "I've seen plenty. Some of my best friends are poltergeists, in fact."

In truth, the only times she'd seen them before were on ghost trains, but she didn't think anyone would be impressed by that.

Poisonous Penelope stepped forward and jabbed Maud's chest with her bony finger. The large werewolf next to her lurched at Maud and growled again.

"What sort of monster are you anyway?" asked Penelope. "I don't remember Batty mentioning it."

All around the graveyard, other pupils

stopped what they were doing and stared towards Maud. Suddenly it was really quiet.

"I can't believe you don't know," said Maud. "I'm the scariest kind of monster in the world."

Penelope looked unimpressed. "And what kind of monster is that exactly?"

Maud looked around. The pupils stared back. She tried to think of the scariest name she could, but nothing came.

"I'm a … Tutu." Well, it would have to do.

The pupils looked confused.

"I'm a terrifying Tutu. The most terrifying one of all, in fact. The other Tutus call me 'Monstrous Maud'."

"I've never heard of a Tutu," said Poisonous Penelope. "Prove it."

Maud fished around in her inside pocket, her heart racing. She usually kept a few plastic bugs in there, and she thought they might come in useful now. She could chuck a cockroach in her mouth and pretend to chew it, or maybe even throw a spider at Penelope and shout, "Boo!" But something was wrong today. In her pocket, she could feel Quentin … and something else soft and fluffy.

Maud pulled it out. To her horror, she saw that it was a tiny doll in a frilly pink evening gown. In her rush to get ready this morning, she must have picked up Milly's blazer by mistake! And now all the Rotwood pupils were going to tease her for being as pathetic as her sister.

Maud looked up, expecting to see a circle of jeering faces. But, to her surprise, the Rotwood students were all staring at the doll with expressions of terror. Even Poisonous Penelope was backing away from it, as though she thought the doll would bite her head off.

Maud didn't understand what was going on, but she wasn't about to miss her chance to scare Penelope. She jumped forward and thrust the doll in the witch's face.

"Raaahhhh! RAAAHHHH!"

Penelope darted away, screaming at the top of her voice. Even the huge werewolf ran after her, yelping with terror.

Maud examined the doll. How on earth had something so boring managed to scare so many monsters?

"Put that horrible thing away!"

Maud looked up to see a teacher running over to her.

"Pupils aren't allowed to scare each other during break. Save it for Fright Classes or you'll end up in the Head's office."

Once again, the mention of the Head's name drew gasps of fear from all the pupils.

"Why's everyone so scared of the Head?" she asked, once the teacher had moved on.

There was an awkward moment of silence, then Paprika said, "You don't want to know."

"Sorry about my brother Warren," said Wilf. "He's a bit of an idiot when it comes to choosing friends."

"That's okay," said Maud. She couldn't believe the bigger werewolf was Wilf's brother. They were certainly as hairy as each other, but Wilf was so much nicer than the snarling, growling wolf who hung around with Penelope.

"That was so monstrous!" said Paprika. "I've never seen Wilf and Penelope so scared before. They chose the wrong person to mess with this time."

"Yeah, totally, er … monstrous," said Maud. She was starting to think that at Rotwood, 'monstrous' might mean something good. "That's what you get for picking on a Tutu."

The others nodded at this and looked impressed. Somehow, she'd managed to convince all these genuine monsters that she was one of them.

As Maud made her way back to the classroom for afternoon lessons, her mind was racing. Maybe she would be able to stay at Rotwood after all. If she could scare the monsters in the playground, who was to say that she couldn't scare Mr Von Bat?

That was decided, then. She was going to do it. She didn't know how, but she would find a way to stay at Rotwood – whatever it took.

Chapter Seven

At lunchtime Maud followed the other pupils down a steep staircase and along a narrow passageway to the school cafeteria, which was inside a dark crypt. It looked like somewhere you'd find lost treasure rather than food, with cobwebs dangling from the low ceiling and dusty lanterns burning on the wall. Rickety benches and wooden tables were laid out across the uneven floor and, at the end of the room, a row of dinner ladies with long, crooked noses and pointed black hats stood behind bubbling cauldrons of food.

"Grub's up!" shouted one of the dinner ladies.

Maud picked up a tray and walked over to them.

"Fried fingernails?" asked the first, offering her a scoop of nails in breadcrumb coating.

"No, thanks," said Maud, and moved along.

"Slime soup?" asked the second dinner lady, offering her a ladleful of thick green liquid.

"Er … not today," said Maud.

"Spider stew?" asked the third.

Maud saw that many of the spiders in the stew were still alive, and were trying in vain to climb the steep sides of the cauldron. She shuddered, but said, "No, thanks," as politely as she could.

"Pie?" asked the fourth dinner lady.

Maud nodded, grateful that she'd managed to find something edible.

She found a space on one of the benches and cut into the crust of the pie. She was about to scoop some into her mouth when she noticed movement on the end of her fork and, to her disgust, saw that she was about to eat a wriggling maggot. When she looked down, she saw that the whole pie was full of maggots.

Opposite, the girl with the red eyes was happily crunching through her own helping. "It's not fair," said the girl, with one of the insects still wiggling out of the side of her mouth. "You got loads more than me."

Maud pushed her plate across to her. "Help yourself. I'm not that hungry, actually."

"Are you sure?" asked the girl. "That's so monstrous of you. I love maggot pie. It's my absolute favourite, except for centipede pasties. And earwig samosas."

"I know how you feel, Tutu girl," said the skeleton boy, who was sitting next to Maud. "I can't eat the food here either. It goes right through me."

To demonstrate, he poured a spoonful of slime soup into his mouth. It dribbled through his jawbone and down on to his ribcage. Maud laughed along with everyone, even though she felt a little sick.

Paprika sat down on the other side of her, carrying a packed lunch, and Maud made a mental note to bring one of her own the very next day.

"Here," said Paprika, offering Maud a stick of celery from his lunch box. "You can have some of my food, if you like."

"Thanks." Maud checked the celery for creepy-crawlies before biting into it. Celery wasn't exactly Maud's favourite food, but at least it didn't squirm when she bit into it.

"I didn't know vampires liked celery," she said. "I thought you drank blood."

"We do," said Paprika. "At least, we're supposed to. I don't really, er ... like it, though. I'm sort of a vegetarian. Dad says I'll get the taste for it one day. He says it will make me big and strong like him."

Maud looked over at the teachers' table, where Mr Von Bat was slurping a bowl of gloopy red liquid through a straw. It looked awful, but she didn't want to say that to Paprika in case it hurt his feelings.

*＊ ✦ ✶ ☆ ★ ✳ ˌ

After lunch, it was time for Maud's first ever Fright Class. She sat right at the front and jotted down everything Mr Von Bat said. This was way better than listening to endless lists of vampire dynasties. And, more importantly, it might help her figure out how to scare Mr Von Bat himself.

"Frightening people is very simple," said Mr Von Bat. "It can be as easy as finding out what someone dislikes, and exploiting their weakness. Take my son, Paprika, for example."

Paprika's pale cheeks blushed as everyone in

the class turned to look at him.

"Paprika is a vampire. And what don't vampires like?"

"Garlic," answered everyone at once.

"Exactly," said Mr Von Bat. He reached into his desk drawer and produced a clove of garlic.

As soon as he saw it, Paprika whimpered with fear and dived under his desk.

Poisonous Penelope let out a loud snort of laughter from the back of the room.

"So here we see the basic fright process in action. The weakness is garlic, and my son's cowardly response was to hide under the desk in terror."

Maud couldn't believe Mr Von Bat was being so mean to his own son. He certainly wouldn't like it if she scared him in front of everyone. Not that he seemed to be frightened of anything, anyway. He didn't even flinch at the garlic, and he was much more of a vampire than Paprika was.

Maud gulped. *Oh no,* she thought. *This is going to be even harder than I expected.*

On the bus home, Maud looked over her notes from Fright Class.

"Look!" said Poisonous Penelope from the seat behind. "Maud can't wait to do her homework."

Warren, who was sitting next to her, gave a chuckling growl.

Maud ignored them, determined to work out what she could do to frighten Mr Von Bat. He'd said that you have to use someone's weakness against them, so how could she do that? She already knew that garlic wouldn't work.

As the bus trundled back through the old forest, Maud stared out of the window at the thick clumps of trees with their withered branches and knotty roots, thinking hard.

And by the time the bus pulled up at her stop, she had a whole page of ideas.

As soon as she got inside, Maud ran upstairs to work on her scaring plans. But she'd only got halfway up when her mum and dad popped out of the living room.

"So how was it?" asked her mum.

"It was fine," said Maud. She wanted to say, "It was amazing," but she didn't want them to know too much about Rotwood. If they found who the other students were, they might not want her to stay.

"I know the first day at a new school can be frightening," said her dad.

You can say that again, thought Maud.

Milly flounced into the hall with her tutu on, practising her ballet steps. "How was Rotwood?" she asked, putting on a fake sympathetic voice because their parents were there. "I've heard it's a frightful place."

"Hmm," said Maud, smiling to herself.

Milly broke off from her prancing and narrowed her eyes.

Maud realised she needed to be more careful. Hiding the truth from her parents wouldn't be a problem. Her mum was working hard on her Dracula musical and her dad was too obsessed with his cars to notice much. But Milly could always sense when Maud was keeping something fun secret, and she always did her best to spoil it.

"I'd better get on with my homework," said Maud.

Mr and Mrs Montague looked up. "Er … pardon?" said her mum.

"Are you feeling all right?" asked her dad.

But Maud was already racing up the stairs. On the way, Maud passed the long diagonal row of Montague family portraits. They showed her parents, grandparents, uncles and aunts, all of them with the same awkward smile and large round glasses.

Maud stopped on the landing, by the photograph of her great-aunt Ethel. She'd never known her great-aunt but, for some reason, Maud felt that Ethel was her kind of person. Perhaps it was her mischievous grin or the twinkle in her eye. Perhaps it was the fact that she was dressed all in black, holding a cat and standing in a graveyard. The cat was completely black apart from a single white paw.

Maud wished she could have met her while she was alive. Ethel would have probably been able to think of hundreds of ways to scare Mr Von Bat. As it was, Maud would just have to keep trying to work it out on her own.

She was going to scare her vampire teacher, if it was the last thing she did.

Chapter Eight

When she arrived at school the next morning, Maud dashed straight up the stairs to Mr Von Bat's classroom, clutching a huge sports bag. Inside was everything she needed to scare Mr Von Bat.

There was no one in the room when Maud arrived. Perfect. She pulled out a vampire mask and cape that her mum had made for the Dracula musical. Then she crouched down behind her teacher's desk and waited.

Two minutes later, Maud heard the door open. She leapt up, flinging her arms out wide and roaring at the top of her voice.

Mr Von Bat calmly took off his cape and hung it on a hook on the wall. "Vampires don't roar," he said. "We hiss. And if that was your attempt to scare me, I'm afraid you'll have to try a teensy bit harder."

"Oh," said Maud. "Sorry."

She took her seat for that morning's Monsterography lesson about the effect of climate on werewolf populations. All through the class, Maud pretended to take notes on Mr Von Bat's lengthy description of a werewolf pack in Alaska. But really, she was making a new list of scaring ideas.

When the bell tolled, Maud left the classroom with the rest of the pupils. But instead of following them down the spiral staircase and into the graveyard, she hid out of sight in a corner until everyone else was gone. Then she blew out all the candles in the corridor, leaving it in pitch blackness.

A moment later, Maud heard Mr Von Bat walk out of the room and shut the door behind him. She grabbed a sheet out of her bag and flung it over her head.

"Woooo!" shouted Maud in her best spooky voice. "WOOOO-OOOO!"

Mr Von Bat sighed. "I meet ghosts every day of the week," he said. "And most of them are extremely boring. How could you possibly think that dressing up as one could frighten me? And who's ever heard of a pink ghost?"

Maud realised it had been a mistake to use one of Milly's sheets as a costume.

"Sorry, Sir," she said.

"Now relight those candles at once or I'll give you a detention," said Mr Von Bat. "And then you'll really have something to moan about."

✳ ✳ ✳ ✩ ★ ✳

At lunchtime Maud didn't go with the other kids to the crypt. Instead she went outside, found a grave covered in soft moss and sat down to eat her packed lunch. She liked most things about Rotwood, but she was happy to give the food a miss.

Nothing she'd tried so far had even made Mr Von Bat break into a sweat. How exactly did you scare a monster like him?

She was no closer to working it out when she looked up to see Paprika and Wilf approaching. The werewolf was clutching a net of marbles.

"Fancy a game?"

Maud stared at the marbles. They stared back, turning as one to look at her. They were eyeballs, she realised.

"Er … I'll just watch you," she said.

"Suit yourself," said Wilf. He opened the net and began to roll the eyeballs along a collapsed headstone.

In the distance she could see the boy with

rotten grey skin from her class staring at them.

"Do you think he wants to come over and talk to us?" asked Maud. "He looks very lonely."

"Who, Zombie Zak?" asked Wilf. "No, that's just what he likes doing. Creeping up on people really slowly and then shouting, 'Ug!' Every monster enjoys different things, you know."

"What do Tutus enjoy best?" asked Paprika. "If you don't mind talking about it, that is."

"Scaring people," said Maud. She felt guilty about lying to her friends. She wanted to tell them she was just an ordinary human girl, but she didn't know how they'd react. They were fine with zombies, werewolves, witches and every other type of spooky creature. But still, she was a human and this was supposed to be a school for monsters.

"It was monstrous when you scared Poisonous Penelope yesterday," said Wilf. "The look on her face was classic."

"Well, that's what we Tutus do," said Maud.

"Ug!" grunted Zombie Zak, who'd finally reached them.

After lunch, Maud, Wilf and Paprika made their way upstairs for afternoon Fright Class. But as they were walking along the murky corridor leading up to Mr Von Bat's classroom, Poisonous Penelope and Warren stepped out of the shadows and blocked Maud's path.

"Hey Tutu!" said Penelope. "If you're so scary, I dare you to go in there." She pointed to a heavy metal door with **DO NOT ENTER** written on it in menacing red letters.

"Don't listen to her," said Paprika. "That's Dad's private blood store. The only people allowed inside are him and the Head."

"But that's nothing for a terrifying Tutu to worry about," said Penelope.

"It's not safe in there," said Paprika. He was fiddling nervously with his cape now. "That's why Dad makes sure it's locked at all times, and he keeps the key in his inside cloak pocket. You're not really thinking of going in, are you?"

Maud considered it for a minute. She wanted to show Penelope she wasn't afraid, but Paprika seemed really worried, and she didn't want to upset him.

"No," said Maud, at last. "I don't really feel like it."

"Looks like the big bad Tutu is too scared to go into that room," said Penelope.

She cackled nastily, and Warren leaned forward and barked in Maud's face.

Maud pushed past the pair of them and continued to the classroom, with Wilf and Paprika in tow.

"Sorry about my brother," said Wilf. "If Mum knew he'd barked in someone's face like that, she'd ground him for the next three full moons.

She always says, just because we're beasts, it doesn't mean we have to be beastly."

"I don't mind him," said Maud. "He's just copying Penelope. She's the one who doesn't like me."

"I wouldn't worry about her," said Wilf. "She's just jealous because she used to be the scariest girl in the school until you came along."

"I suppose so," said Maud, feeling guilty about her lie again.

Maud knew that Penelope had only dared her to go inside the blood storage room to get her in trouble, but still, it made her wonder. Why was Mr Von Bat so particular about keeping it locked all the time? Was he worried about pupils snacking on the blood?

Whatever the reason, it wasn't important now. Maud had to concentrate on scaring her teacher. All the Rotwood students were getting their books out, ready for Fright Class. Quickly, Maud went over to her locker to fetch Quentin.

"Sorry, Quentin," she said. "But I need your help for a few minutes."

The rat leapt into Maud's blazer pocket, quivering with fear.

"Oh, don't worry," said Maud. "It's nothing dangerous."

Maud crept to the front of the classroom, placed Quentin carefully in Mr Von Bat's desk drawer and returned to her seat.

A couple of minutes later, Mr Von Bat strode into the room and began Fright Class. Today it was all about the practice of voodoo magic. He paced up and down the room, detailing complicated ancient rituals. Every time he walked past his desk drawer, Maud willed him to open it. She thought of the chaos at Primrose Towers, and imagined the whole class, including Mr Von Bat, screaming and panicking.

It seemed to take for ever, but at last Mr Von Bat paused next to the drawer. "Now, I have an example of a voodoo doll here."

This is it, thought Maud, willing Quentin to leap out at Mr Von Bat.

"It's in here somewhere," said Mr Von Bat, searching around in his drawer.

Quentin scuttled out of the drawer and on to the desk. Mr Von Bat glanced at him for a second, then went right back to rooting in his drawer. Unfortunately, he didn't seem very shocked. Quentin, on the other hand, ran straight back to Maud. He leapt back into her blazer pocket and sat there, shaking.

"Sorry, Quentin," Maud whispered. "I didn't mean to scare you. I wanted you to give the teacher a fright, not the other way round. But I suppose he does look pretty fearsome with his fangs and his cape."

Quentin stuck his head out of Maud's pocket and looked around the room. Paprika, who was sitting next to Maud, spotted him.

"Oh, wow!" he said. "You've got a rat! What's his name?"

"Quentin."

"Can I hold him?"

"Um ... you can try. But he's very nervous around new people."

Paprika picked Quentin out of Maud's pocket and stroked his fur. This caught the attention of the rest of the class, who gathered round to look. Quentin trembled with fear. *He's so scared he can't move*, thought Maud.

"He's so cool," said a voice next to her that must have been Invisible Isabel.

"I don't see the big deal," said Poisonous Penelope. "My uncle keeps rats twice that size. And they carry the plague."

"Stop that at once," shouted Mr Von Bat from the front of the room. "This is a classroom, not a petting zoo."

Quentin darted back into Maud's pocket.

Mr Von Bat held up a straw doll and a sharp pin. "The next person who decides to disrupt the class gets to be the volunteer in my voodoo demonstration."

The pupils zoomed back to their seats and faced the front.

Mr Von Bat set them all extra homework as punishment for the disruption. Everyone groaned, but Maud thought the essay title he gave them, "The Scariest Thing in the World", was quite exciting.

✳ ★ ✶ ☆ ★ ✳ ⋆

"Drat," muttered Maud, as she stared out of the window at the dark forest on the bus home. Nothing she'd tried on Mr Von Bat had worked. Not the vampire costume, not the ghost costume, not even her pet rat. Maybe she should just accept that Mr Von Bat really was fright proof.

Quentin peered up from inside her blazer pocket.

"You mustn't blame yourself, Quentin," said Maud. "It's all my fault."

Clearly, the things that used to scare the girls at Primrose Towers wouldn't work at Rotwood. So what would? The only thing that had frightened anyone so far was … Of course! Why hadn't she seen it sooner?

Maud had an idea. And by the time she stepped off the creaking bus, the idea had turned into a plan.

Chapter Nine

The next morning, Maud waited for Milly to go to the bathroom for her daily washing routine. Then she sneaked across to her sister's lilac chest of drawers and rooted around inside.

If the pupils at Rotwood loved all the things that the pupils at Primrose Towers were scared of, did that mean the opposite was true? Maybe the doll she'd brought on her first day wasn't the only soppy thing that would terrify the Rotwood monsters. For once, Maud was pleased her sister owned so much silly pink stuff.

A few minutes later, Maud raced out of the

house with a bag full of Milly's possessions and a cardboard box with breathing holes and something wriggling around inside. Luckily for her, the Rotwood bus arrived before her sister caught up with her.

When she got to school, Maud lurked in the corridor outside Mr Von Bat's classroom as the other pupils went in. As soon as she heard him taking the morning register, she changed into Milly's ballet costume, complete with pink frilly tutu, white tights, satin shoes and rosebud hair clips. Then she took a deep breath, and flounced into the classroom.

Remembering the moves she'd seen her sister practising, Maud stretched out her arms, lifted up one knee and whirled around on her other foot. It wasn't a very graceful pirouette, but it did the trick.

All around the room, pupils jumped out of their seats and screamed at the tops of their voices. Oscar reached out to his detached head, on the desk in front of him, and covered his eyes. Poisonous Penelope screeched so hard her hat fell off, and then dived into the cupboard at the back of the classroom. Even Wilf let out a yelp of fright.

Maud looked across to Mr Von Bat. Surely, this must have got to him. He just stared at her with his arms folded.

"Change back into your uniform at once," he said. "You look ridiculous."

Maud sighed. Her pirouette had terrified everyone except the one person it was aimed at.

At lunchtime, Maud took the cardboard box down to the cafeteria and hid it under the table, keeping an eye on the door for Mr Von Bat.

As soon as he came in, she lifted the box up on to the table, pulled the sticky tape off the flaps and tipped it on its side.

Milly's pet bunny, Lollipop, flopped out. She had white fur, floppy brown ears and a neat pink bow on the top of her head. She sniffed at the air with her tiny pink nose and began to hop along the table.

A shrill chorus of shrieks rose up in the cafeteria as the pupils spotted the bunny. Paprika was so frightened he turned into a bat and swooped around the room. Several other pupils ran to the back of the hall in panic, overturning the food cauldrons. Swamp soup spilled around the dinner ladies' ankles.

Maud was staring at Mr Von Bat, desperate for him to scream. And … Yes! His face was pale and he was fidgeting around uncomfortably. *This is it*, thought Maud. But then Lollipop shuffled right past him and he simply glanced down and tutted.

Maud looked around to work out what had made Mr Von Bat look so queasy. The floor was covered in gloopy puddles of bug stew, blood soup and worm Bolognese. But why would that make him uncomfortable?

Maud tempted Lollipop back into the box with a lettuce leaf and hid it under the table before anyone noticed who'd unleashed the beast.

She looked up just in time to see Paprika turn back into a vampire in a huge puff of smoke and tumble right down into a cauldron of slug surprise. One of the dinner ladies tugged him out and dumped him on the floor, his cape dripping and wriggling behind him.

"Look at you," she said, picking a large slug off his shoulder.

*˙ ★ ✳ ✰ ★ ✳ ˳

In that afternoon's Fright Class, everyone had to read out their essays about the scariest thing in the world. It was Maud's last chance of the day to scare her teacher.

Poisonous Penelope wrote about a spell that turned people to stone and Invisible Isabel spoke about a candlelit séance. Zombie Zak talked about a time that he and his friends slowly surrounded a secluded house in a forest and shouted, "Ug!" Oscar had written about the time his body left him at home by mistake and he missed a family trip to the seaside.

When it came to Maud's turn, she took Milly's perfumed notebook out of her satchel and opened it. Around the classroom, several pupils winced as glitter and gold stars spilled out on to the floor.

Maud cleared her throat. "My essay is called 'One hundred reasons why I love Mr Snuggly Boo'. Number one: I love my teddy because his fur is so soft and kissable. Number two: I love my teddy because he smells of sweet summer blossom …"

As Maud read through the list, she saw that everyone was wide-eyed with fear. Poisonous Penelope was trembling and biting her nails. Invisible Isabel was so scared she tried to sneak out of the classroom, but Mr Von Bat noticed the door opening on its own and sent her back to her seat.

"… Number fifty: I love my teddy because he has a little red love heart sewn on his chest …"

By the time Maud got to sixty, most pupils were sobbing with fear and begging her to stop. Paprika was even paler than normal, and Oscar took off his head and put it inside his desk so he wouldn't have to hear any more.

"… Number one hundred: and most of all I love my teddy because he is so generous and kind to all the other bears in Snuggly Boo Woods!" Maud looked up at Mr Von Bat.

"Well," he said, "I don't see what's so scary

about that. I'm giving you an F minus. And you're lucky to get that."

"Drat," muttered Maud, as she shoved the notebook back into her bag.

"I got an A for mine," said Poisonous Penelope. "I'd have thought a terrifying Tutu like you would have got an A plus."

"I thought it was frightening," said Paprika. "And you looked pretty scared too. You were trembling so much you made your desk shake."

"At least I didn't turn into a bat and end up covered in slugs at lunchtime," snapped Poisonous Penelope.

Paprika blushed with shame, but Maud smiled at him. It was good to see him standing up to Poisonous Penelope for once, even if she was right about the slugs.

When Maud got home that evening, she put Milly's bunny back in her hutch, then sneaked upstairs to return Milly's ballet clothes and notebook. Luckily, she'd just managed to put everything back when her sister burst in.

"I need this room tonight," said Milly. "I'll be practising my ballet in here, for the big show. You'll have to find somewhere else to do whatever disgusting stuff you want to do."

Maud didn't have the energy to argue, so she went downstairs to the living room. But when she got there, she found that every chair was covered in patches of material and sewing patterns.

"Hello, dear," said Maud's mum, without looking up from the flouncy dress she was stitching.

Maud tried the dining room, but her dad had laid out all his tools in alphabetical order to check them.

"This is a lovely torque wrench," he said,

pointing to a tool with an adjustable handle. "You wouldn't believe I've had that since 1997, would you?"

"No, Dad," Maud said, and left before he started talking about cars.

She went to fetch Quentin and then settled down on the stairs for the evening. Milly was stomping hard on the floor above them, which made Quentin quiver with anxiety.

"Oh, Quentin," said Maud. "I wish Mr Von Bat was frightened as easily as you."

She thought back to her very first Fright Class. Mr Von Bat had said you should find out what someone's weakness is and use it against them. But Mr Von Bat didn't have a weakness. Everything she'd tried, from the spooky to the soppy, had failed. So what was left?

Maud was running out of time. She had two more days to scare Mr Von Bat, or she'd have to find another school. If there were any that would take her.

Her eyes were drawn to the portrait of her great-aunt Ethel once again. She looked so confident in her moonlit graveyard. She'd have known what to do.

A scream rang out from Maud and Milly's bedroom.

"Mum!" shouted Milly. "Maud's been going through my chest of drawers again! And she's been looking through my notebook! And she's been wearing my ballet clothes! You have to do something about it!"

Just when she'd thought things couldn't get any worse.

Chapter Ten

The next morning, Maud spent all of Vampire History staring at Mr Von Bat and wondering what his weakness could be. She was supposed to be reading a passage from her textbook about the causes of the Great Vampire War of 1823. But she was too preoccupied to take in the history of the Bitesworthys and the Bludhaus-Essenbergs.

"Ouch!" shouted Paprika from the desk next to her. He'd given himself a paper cut on his textbook and was holding out his finger to show his dad.

Mr Von Bat grimaced. "Go to the sick room at once. I'm not a nurse."

"I'll take him," said Maud.

"Very well," said Mr Von Bat. "But no messing around. And make sure you get that cut properly covered up."

The school sick room was a small, dusty chamber with a broken bed at each end and a table full of what looked like medieval torture instruments in the middle. A huge green ogre was standing in the middle of the room, wearing an apron covered in dark stains. Maud was just about to ask if the ogre knew where the nurse was when she read its badge. It *was* the nurse.

She hoped she never got ill in school.

The ogre wrapped Paprika's finger in a dirty bandage and grunted to say that it was finished.

As they walked back along a murky corridor to the classroom, Maud thought about how Mr Von Bat had reacted to the drop of blood on Paprika's finger. The only other time she'd seen him make a face like that was when he'd seen the overturned cauldrons in the cafeteria.

Maud paused in the corridor. "Didn't you think your dad was a bit funny about that cut?" she asked Paprika.

"Not really," he said. "He gets like that sometimes."

"Which times?" asked Maud.

Paprika looked like he was about to say something, but seemed to stop himself. "None in particular. It's pretty random, really."

As they walked back to the classroom, they passed Mr Von Bat's blood storage cupboard again. Maud looked at the **DO NOT ENTER** sign and found herself wondering about the room again.

When they got back into the classroom, Maud picked Quentin up from her pencil case, where he'd been sleeping, and popped him into her pocket. Then she waited for Mr Von Bat to get distracted. After a while, Oscar put up his hand and asked for help with the questions about the vampire war. He was scratching his decapitated head with his other hand, clearly struggling with it all.

"Please may I go to the toilet, Sir?" asked Maud.

"If you must," said Mr Von Bat. "You just can't sit still today, can you?"

As Maud passed the coat hooks, she slipped her hand into the inside pocket of her teacher's cape and grabbed the key she found there.

After a short jog down the corridor, she was outside the door to the blood storage room. Glancing at the **DO NOT ENTER** sign one last time, she turned the key in the lock and pushed open the door.

"Okay, Quentin," she said. "You keep a lookout."

Quentin took up position outside the doorway, glancing from left to right and lifting his snout in the air.

Inside the room was a small stock cupboard full of jars of blood, just as Paprika had said.

Maud felt goose bumps all over. It was probably just because she was feeling guilty about ignoring the sign. But at the same time, she couldn't shake the feeling that she was being watched. What if there was a CCTV camera in here? Maud looked around. She didn't see how there could be. Pencil sharpeners and rulers were about as far as technology went in Rotwood; there was no way they would have something as advanced as cameras.

Maud took down one of the jars. She should have freaked out at holding a jar of actual human blood, but she pretended it was tomato juice, and then it didn't seem so bad.

She unscrewed the top. The liquid didn't smell much like blood at all. It had a savoury odour that was strangely familiar. Maud dipped a finger into it and lifted it cautiously to her nose.

What?

She licked her finger.

Maud didn't have to pretend the blood was tomato juice. It *was* tomato juice.

Maud couldn't believe it. So Mr Von Bat wasn't a fearsome blood-drinker after all. He was a vegetarian, just like Paprika.

Carefully, she placed the jar back on the shelf and locked the door. Then she scooped Quentin back into her pocket and ran to the classroom.

When she got back, Maud was relieved to see that Mr Von Bat was busy trying to help Zombie Zak. He was explaining the questions in the textbook, but Zak just kept looking at him and saying, "Ug." Maud slipped Mr Von Bat's key into his cape and returned to her seat.

A few minutes later, Mr Von Bat came over and pointed to her textbook. "And have we worked it all out yet?" he asked.

Maud smiled and nodded, although she was none the wiser about whether the Bitesworthys or the Bludhaus-Essenbergs started the Great Vampire War. But she did think she might finally have worked out how to scare her vampire teacher. Tomorrow she would try one more time. And this time it was going to work.

It had to.

Milly was practising her twirls and leaps in their bedroom again that night.

"Go away, Maud," she said. "My big show's tomorrow, remember?"

"That's okay," said Maud. "I was planning on spending tonight in the kitchen anyway. Which reminds me, do you still have the recipe for the cake you made for Miss Bloom last Friday?"

Milly froze, mid-pirouette. "Why would you be interested?" she asked suspiciously. "You hate baking."

"I just thought I'd give it a try."

"It's a very difficult recipe. You probably won't be able to follow it."

"I could always stay up here with you instead, if you prefer. I could help you out with your ballet?"

Milly made a face and went straight to her bookcase. She handed Maud a book called *The Magical Princess's Guide to Yummy Baking*.

"Don't spill anything on it," said Milly. "And promise it won't go near any bugs, worms or maggots, or I'll tell, and I'll never lend you anything ever again."

"I promise," said Maud, and ran down to the kitchen.

Maud turned to the section on Special Cakes for Magical People and found the one Milly had made for Miss Bloom. She measured out the exact amounts of eggs, butter, flour and sugar and followed the instructions precisely. Except for one or two minor adjustments.

When the cake was baked, she traced out the words "Best Teacher Ever" in purple icing, and stood back to admire her work. It looked a little messier than when Milly had done it – but you could still read it clearly.

A couple of minutes later, Mrs Montague came into the kitchen for a drink of water. When she saw the cake, she dropped the glass she was carrying. *SMASH!*

"Oh my goodness!" she gasped.

"What is it now?" asked Mr Montague, running into the kitchen.

"Maud hasn't put her ant jar on the spice rack again, has she?" asked Milly, following him in.

Maud's dad was staring at the cake, eyes bulging behind his glasses. "Well done, Maud," he managed to say, at last. "That cake is … lovely. It looks like Rotwood really is changing you for the better." And he leaned down to give Maud a big hug.

"Thanks," said Maud, blushing.

"It was *my* recipe," said Milly. "She got the recipe from my book."

The next morning, Maud got ready early and waited by the door for her sister. At last, Milly twirled out on to the landing in her full ballet costume.

Their parents came out into the hallway to admire Milly, who curtseyed for them.

"What a lovely tutu," said their mum.

"Thanks," said Milly.

"Thanks," said Maud.

Milly looked at her with confusion.

"Good luck with your big day," said their dad.

"Thanks," said Milly.

"Thanks," said Maud.

Milly narrowed her eyes.

✳ ✦ ✳ ✧ ✦ ✳

On the bus, Maud held her cake box flat on her lap, willing the old wreck to trundle faster along the forest road. As soon it pulled up in the clearing, Maud dashed straight into Rotwood and up the winding staircase to her classroom.

Mr Von Bat looked up from the *Vampire Times* crossword as she burst in. "Good morning," he said, setting down his quill. "Or should I say, 'Good bye'? Didn't get very far with the scaring in the end, did we? What a shame. I was just starting to get used to having you around."

"Never mind," said Maud. "I tried my best."

Mr Von Bat smiled. "So it appears it's your last day at Rotwood, then."

"I know," said Maud. "That's why I've brought in something for you. It's to thank you for teaching me so well." Maud opened the cake tin.

A broad grin stretched across Mr Von Bat's face. "Best teacher ever? Well, if you say so.

I suppose I could treat myself to a piece. To celebrate my little victory."

Maud took out a knife from her bag and sliced into the cake. As she did so, thick red liquid oozed out.

Mr Von Bat looked at it with growing panic. "What … what's that?" he asked.

"It's a blood cake, of course," said Maud. "What other sort of cake would I make for a vampire?" She lifted the slice out and more red stuff splattered down on to Mr Von Bat's desk.

Mr Von Bat jumped up and backed away from the cake, growing paler by the second.

Maud grinned. She'd spent ages making sure the runny red icing looked exactly like blood. It was perfect.

"I hope you like it," she said, thrusting the slice towards Mr Von Bat. "I made it just for you."

Mr Von Bat backed up to the wall, but Maud went after him, holding the slice right up to his face. A drop of the red icing splashed on to Mr Von Bat's cape and he let out a shriek of terror. Then he cowered on the floor, covering his head with his hands.

"You're not scared, are you?" asked Maud, innocently.

"Urgh! Get that thing away from me!" he shouted. "I hate blood!"

Maud calmly put the slice back in the cake box. "I thought as much," she said. "You're frightened of blood, just like Paprika. Aren't vampires supposed to like it?"

"All right, all right," he said. "You win." Mr Von Bat reached into his mouth and pulled out a pair of false fangs.

Chapter Eleven

Maud stared at Mr Von Bat's plastic teeth. What on earth was going on?

"So you're … not a real vampire?" she asked.

Mr Von Bat couldn't look her in the eye. "No," he said glumly. "I'm as human as you are."

Maud put the cake back in the tin and helped Mr Von Bat to his feet again. He didn't look very strict or frightening any more. In fact, he looked as if he might be sick at any moment. Maud had thought she'd be over the moon if she managed to scare her teacher, but he looked so petrified that she felt bad about it instead.

"And what about Paprika?" asked Maud.

"He's half-vampire," replied Mr Von Bat as he straightened out his cape. "His mum's one, you see."

No wonder Paprika found it so hard to be a fearsome creature of the night. Maud felt sorry for him now, too.

"Does he know?" she asked.

"Yes, but he'd never tell anyone. He knows I'd get thrown out of Rotwood. And the truth is, I really like it here."

"Me too."

"The school I used to teach in was so horrible, with polished floors and rows of computers and large windows. I suppose the pupils were better behaved, but it was all just so … normal." Mr Von Bat shuddered at the memory.

"I know exactly what you mean," said Maud.

"Of course you do. You're human too. That's why I didn't want you around. I thought you'd guess the truth about me and I'd have to go back to somewhere nasty and ordinary."

Maud heard footsteps coming up the winding staircase. It was time for morning lessons.

"You won't tell anyone, will you?" asked Mr Von Bat.

"Of course not," said Maud. "Providing you let me stay at Rotwood, that is."

Mr Von Bat sighed. "Very well then. Just get rid of that revolting cake."

Maud wondered if she should explain, but decided not to. After all, it was a delicious cake and now she had lots of new friends to share it with. She stuffed it into her desk while Mr Von Bat put his fangs back in and recovered his stern expression.

The door opened, and Class 3B filed in.

At break, Maud lifted Quentin out of her pencil case into her pocket and went out to the graveyard. She spotted Paprika in the corner, rolling eyeball marbles along a cracked tombstone. She went over to him.

"Hi Paprika," she said. "I think I ought to tell you something."

"Is it about Tutus?"

"No, it's about your dad. I, er … I know he's a human."

Paprika's eyes widened and Maud began to worry that he was going to turn into a bat again.

"It's okay," she said. "The secret's safe with me. After all, we're friends, aren't we?"

Paprika nodded and breathed a sigh of relief. "How did you find out? Can you read minds? Is that one of the special powers Tutus have?"

"No," said Maud. "It's nothing like that. In fact, that's the other thing I wanted to tell you. I'm not a Tutu at all. There's no such creature. I just made it up because … well … because I'm just a normal human too."

Paprika looked confused. "But humans aren't allowed in this school."

"I know," said Maud. "But you'll keep my secret if I keep yours, won't you?"

"Of course I will." He smiled, showing his stunted, half-vampire fangs. "It's like you said – we're friends. I'm glad you're here, Maud. You're so monstrous."

Maud smiled back, and looked out over the misty graveyard. *Her* misty graveyard. In the distance, she could see a group of pupils playing football. Zombie Zak was in goal, but he couldn't move fast enough to catch the ball.

"Actually, I'm pleased you're a human," Paprika said. "Sometimes when my friends are doing amazing things like taking off their heads and casting spells, I feel a little … funny about being half-human. But you're human and you're cool, so they can't all be ordinary."

"Not all of us," said Maud. She couldn't

help remembering her family's last holiday to Cornwall, when her dad spent the journey there and back naming the engine type of every passing car.

Maud felt a hand on her shoulder. She looked up to see Mr Von Bat, who looked even paler than when he'd seen the blood cake.

"I'm sorry about this," he said. "But I've just heard that the Head wants to see you."

Maud's heart sank. After all the effort she'd made to convince Mr Von Bat to let her stay, it seemed as though the Head had found out about her.

As Maud made her way back across the playground, she could hear the news spreading.

Wilf ran over. "What did you do?" he asked. "You must be in serious trouble."

"I don't know," Maud lied.

"I told you there was something wrong with her," said Poisonous Penelope. "Whatever she's done, I hope they make an example of her."

Inside, Mr Von Bat pointed Maud in the direction of the Head's office, which was at the end of a long corridor lit by a row of flaming torches.

Maud had to push away cobwebs as she ventured down it. It didn't seem like a part of the school that was used much.

At the end of the corridor was a large door made of oak planks held together by iron studs. The doorknob was in the shape of a skull, and she could hear a yowling sound coming from inside. Whatever kind of monster the Head was, she was sure this wasn't going to be pleasant.

It didn't matter, though. She'd been summoned, and she'd have to face whatever was inside. This was going to be her last day at Rotwood, and it was hopeless fighting it.

Maud knocked on the door and, all by itself, it creaked open.

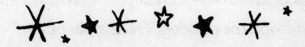

The first things Maud noticed were the cats. There was a fat ginger tom curled up on the windowsill, a grey cat with bright green eyes on top of a cupboard, and a tabby cat prowling around the stone floor.

All of them turned to look at Maud as she entered, and some mewed at her. Quentin cowered inside her pocket.

In the centre of the room was a large wooden desk lit by four dribbling candles and, behind it, the back of a large leather swivel chair.

Maud held her breath as the chair turned slowly round to reveal …

Maud gasped.

Sitting in the chair was a nice-looking elderly woman wearing huge round glasses, her hands stroking a black cat in her lap. Black all but a single white paw.

Maud couldn't believe it. "Great-aunt Ethel!" she gasped.

The woman nodded. "Hello, Maud."

"I thought you were dead," Maud whispered.

"Dead?" said great-aunt Ethel. "Of course I'm dead. Would I be able to do this if I was alive?" She passed her hand right through one of the candles.

"So you're a ghost?"

"Naturally," said Great-aunt Ethel.

"And the Head of Rotwood!"

"Have a seat," said her great-aunt. "I'll explain."

Maud sat down on an antique wooden chair that was covered in claw marks.

"You know, Maud, I've been watching you this week, and I've been very impressed."

Maud beamed with pride. A black cat brushed against her leg, and she stroked its back.

"The way that you scared Mr Von Bat this morning was very clever indeed."

"You saw that?"

The Head grinned. "Didn't the others tell you? I see most things."

"It was nothing, really."

"Every fright counts, that's what we say here," said the Head. "That's the reason I founded this school, you know. To give young monsters a place where they could learn to scare before they go out into the world."

Maud felt very proud to be related to the founder of Rotwood. No wonder she loved it here! And now she knew why she'd never fitted in at Primrose Towers.

"So I must have some monster blood!" she said.

Her great-aunt grinned. "We've all got a few drops of monster in us," she said. "Some just choose to ignore it. I never liked school much when I was a girl. It all seemed so serious and stuffy. I wanted to create the kind of school I'd like to have gone to."

"And you've done a brilliant job," said Maud. "This is the best school I've ever seen."

"Well, thank you for saying so. And let me

just say how delighted I am to have my great-niece here at Rotwood. I think you'll fit in very well. You, Maud Montague, are going to be a truly monstrous monster."

Maud was so happy about being allowed to stay that she wanted to jump up and hug Great-aunt Ethel. But then she remembered that her arms would pass right through her, so she just thanked her great-aunt and left the room.

Chapter Twelve

That evening Maud went to Primrose Towers with her parents to watch Milly's dance class perform their ballet recital in the school hall. The show was every bit as dull as Maud had imagined. Just lots of girls prancing around, looking very serious, in front of a painting of a lake. But Maud was so pleased about being allowed to stay at Rotwood that she didn't mind.

Even when her sister took centre stage to perform the pirouette she'd been practising all week, and then frowned at the audience until they applauded, Maud didn't get annoyed. She just thought about how she'd be seeing her friends Wilf and Paprika again on Monday.

Milly had protested for ages about Maud coming along, of course. She'd said that Maud would find some way to wreck it as usual. But she was wrong. Maud managed to sit peacefully and quietly through the whole thing, and even forced herself to clap at the right moments.

Mrs Montague leaned over to Maud and gave her a tight hug. "I bet you're glad you're not still at Primrose Towers, cupcake," she said. "Tutus aren't really your thing, are they?"

"Oh, they're not that bad," said Maud.

On stage, the dancing seemed to have taken an unexpected turn. One of the girls was pointing at the floor and screaming, while the others clustered at the back of the stage, peering nervously around their feet.

Maud checked her blazer pocket. Quentin had escaped again – probably because all the camera flashes had startled him. Suzie Singh's dancing had become frantic as she hopped across the stage as if it were red hot. With a squeal, she jumped into the arms of her mum, who was sitting in the front row. The rest of the girls were trying to run off the side of the stage, while Miss Bloom was attempting desperately to push them back on. There was no sign of Quentin.

Only Milly was making an effort to go on with the show, performing her pirouette over and over again as the others panicked all around her. In the middle of one of her spins, she knocked into Poppy Simpkins and sent her crashing through the lake backdrop, ripping it in half.

Maud looked down the aisle and was relieved to see Quentin scuttling back towards her. She scooped him back into her pocket, glad that he was safe.

"I thought I told you not to run away like

that," she said, stroking his nose.

Quentin gave a toothy grin and nuzzled her finger.

As Maud settled back to watch the chaos, she thought of her first week at Rotwood. She'd met some nice people and some who were not so nice, but they were all more interesting than the Primrose Towers girls.

Great-aunt Ethel was right, she thought. *I'm going to be a truly monstrous monster.*

Other titles by A. B. Saddlewick:

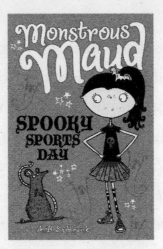

ISBN: 978-1-78055-073-2

Available in August 2012:

Freaky Sleepover
ISBN: 978-1-78055-074-9

School Scare
ISBN: 978-1-78055-075-6